# WHO SAID BOO?

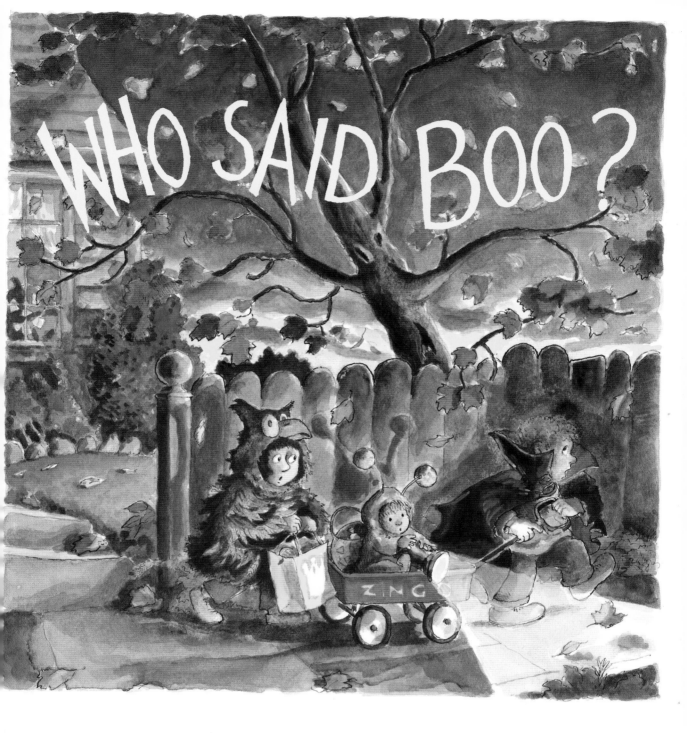

# WHO SAID BOO?

## HALLOWEEN POEMS FOR THE VERY YOUNG

Written by **Nancy White Carlstrom**
Illustrated by **R. W. Alley**

Simon & Schuster Books for Young Readers

For the wonderful students, teachers,
and staff of Woodriver Elementary School.

N. W. C.

To Cassandra, our Tinker Bell,
and Max, our Cowboy.

R. W. A.

SIMON & SCHUSTER BOOKS FOR YOUNG READERS
An imprint of Simon & Schuster Children's Publishing Division
1230 Avenue of the Americas, New York, New York 10020

SIMON & SCHUSTER BOOKS FOR YOUNG READERS
is a trademark of Simon & Schuster.
Designed by Carolyn Boschi
The text of this book is set in 14.5 point Lydian Bold.
The illustrations are rendered in pen and ink and watercolor.
Manufactured in Hong Kong by Dai Nippon
First edition
10 9 8 7 6 5 4 3 2 1

14540

LIBRARY OF CONGRESS CATALOGING-IN-PUBLICATION DATA

Carlstrom, Nancy White.
Who said boo? : Halloween poems for the very young / written by
Nancy White Carlstrom ; illustrated by R. W. Alley.—1st ed.
    p.     cm.
ISBN 0-689-80308-7
Summary: A collection of poems celebrating such Halloween
phenomena as monsters, witches, haunted houses, and jack-o'-lanterns.
1. Halloween—Juvenile poetry.     2. Children's poetry, American.
[1. Halloween—Poetry.     2. American poetry.]
1. Alley, R. W. (Robert W.), ill.     II. Title
PS3553.A7355W48     1995     811'.54—dc20     94-33577

# The Poems

# ON HALLOWEEN NIGHT

This is the way the cat walks
*Pit pat, pit pat*
This is the way the cat walks
On Halloween night.

This is the way the moon walks
*Tip tap, tip tap*
This is the way the moon walks
On Halloween night.

This is the way the kids walk
*Trip trap, trip trap*
This is the way the kids walk
On Halloween night.

This is the way the wind walks
*Rip rap, rip rap*
This is the way the wind walks
On Halloween night.

This is the way the tree walks
*Scritch scratch,
scritch scratch*
This is the way the tree walks
On Halloween night.

*Pit pat
Tip tap
Trip trap
Rip rap
Scritch scratch*

BOO!

# WHO SAID BOO?

BOO!

Did Mama say Boo?
No, Mama said Shoe.

Did Papa say Boo?
No, Papa said Who.

Did Baby say Boo?
No, Baby said Coo.

Did Sister say Boo?
No, Sister said Goo.

Did Brother say Boo?
No, Brother said Chew.

Did Grandpa say Boo?
No, Grandpa said Moo.

Did Granny say Boo?

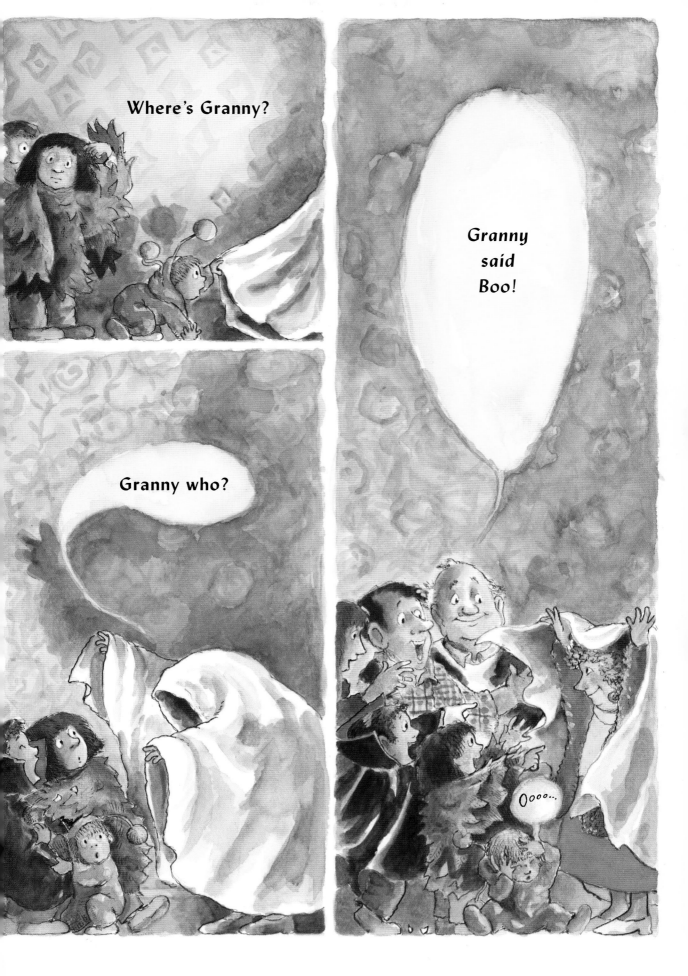

I'm a monster
Be careful

I'm a monster
I can scare you

I'm a monster
If you let me

I'm a monster
I will get you

I'm a monster
In the mirror

*Eeek!*

I don't like what I see
Is that really me?

I'm a monster!

But please
Let me carry my mask!

# MIXED-UP
# MASQUERADE

DRESSING ROOM

Rabbit's nose
Wiggle wiggle
Rabbit's tail
Puffball
Rabbit's paws
Soft fur
Rabbit's ears
Oh no!
Where did they go?

Where are Rabbit's ears?

Pig's tail
Curlicue
Pig's ears
Pink pink
Pig's feet
*Plink plink*
Pig's nose
Oh no!
Where did it go?

Where is Pig's nose?

Pelican's voice
*Squawk squawk*
Pelican's feet
*Clap clap*
Pelican's wings
*Flap flap*
Pelican's beak
Oh no!
Where did it go?

Where is Pelican's beak?

13

Owl's eyes
Wide-open
Owl's beak
Yellow sharp
Owl's ears
Tiny tufts
Owl's feathers
Oh no!
Where did they go?

Where are Owl's feathers?

Bear's stomach
Berry full
Bear's nose
*Sniff snuff*
Bear's growl
*Grrr-rruf*
Bear's paws
Oh no!
Where did they go?

Where are Bear's paws?

Mouse's tail
Teeny-tiny
Mouse's ears
Point up
Mouse's feet
*Scriff scruff*
Mouse's squeak
Oh no!
Where did it go?

Where is Mouse's squeak?

Rabbit ears
Pig nose
Pelican beak
Owl feathers
Bear paws
Mouse squeak
Somebody's sister
In a mixed-up masquerade

squeak

*

# HAUNTED HOUSE

The haunted house
ooo-ooo
Is dark inside
ooo-ooo
Cat eyes glow
ooo-ooo
Bat wings glide
ooo-ooo
Are you afraid?
ooo-ooo

Please come with me
ooo-ooo

I'll take your hand
ooo-ooo
And we can be
ooo-ooo

BOO!

BOO!

BOO!

EEEEEK!

Scared together!

# HALLOWEEN CARNIVAL

I left my wig at the penny toss
My cape is hanging near the door
My gloves are floating in the tub
I'm not a vampire anymore.

I'm Me at the Halloween Carnival!

# HOW MANY WITCHES?

How many witches on a broomstick?
How many black cats creeping by?
How many pumpkins in the garden?
How many full moons in the sky?

4–3–2–1
1–2–3–4

Knock!   Knock!   Knock!   Knock!
Open up the door!

# WHO-O-O ARE YOU?

Click!    Clack!
Click!    Clack!
Who's that walking?

Plip!    Plop!
Plip!    Plop!
Who's that hopping?

Thump!    Bump!
Thump!    Bump!
Who's that jumping?

Click!   Clack!
Plip!   Plop!
Thump!   Bump!
Boo!

Who-o-o are you?

It's the Boo-o-o-o
Bunny!

## SOMEBODY'S TAPPING AT MY WINDOW

Somebody's tapping at my window
Somebody's knocking at the door
Somebody's creaking up the stairs

Somebody's brother snores!

# Bones

Tickle his funny bone
Make him grin
Rattle him, rattle him
Skeleton Jim

# WHO'S AFRAID OF THE BIG BAD SHADOW?

Who's afraid of the big bad shadow?
*Swinging on the wall*
Who's afraid of the big bad footsteps?
*Running down the hall*
Who's afraid of the scratching noise?
*As the wind begins to call*

I am! I am!
Mommy! Mommy!

Oh, Daddy was the shadow
Swinging on the wall
Daddy made the footsteps
Running down the hall
Daddy made the noise
As the wind began to call

Daddy's fixing the furnace
On Halloween night.

# JACK-O'-LANTERNS

Get the pumpkins
Carve a grin
Lift the lid
Put a candle in.

Turn the lights out
Watch them glow
Jack-o'-lanterns
Seem to know

Just what to say
On Halloween night!

Trick or treat!
Good night!